Willa The

Wisp

by DonnaRae Menard

for Bella

Dedicated to my Granddaughter

IZZABELLA DEZZARAE VERRILL

To Ellie
Enjoy the read.
Donnarae Menard
8/13/2022.

With Special Acknowledgment to the

Jackson Woman's Writers Group

Cover by

Mylinda Piadade Graphics

Willa the Wisp

Far down the hill, past the forest, the children played in the schoolyard. From the top of Hurricane Mountain, Willa could see them. She had far sight and watched them play every day. For many years she had watched different children play in the same school yard. While Willa watched the children would swing on the tall metal swings, slid down the slippery slide, and play in the sandbox. She knew each child by name and remembered them even when they were grown and gone.

With her fists clutched together and her shoulders rounded, Willa waited. Danielle ran around the toy shed with Peter running behind her. Peter reached out his long arm toward the racing girl, his hand flexed to tag her and he missed. As he tumbled down, Danielle ran back to the safety of home in the sandbox. Her twinkling laugh carried on the wind to Willa.

"Yes," shouted Willa. She spun around, jumped high and whizzed around the Mulberry bushes three times. "Safe!" She exclaimed. "You may be a big boy, Peter Weathers, but you are not fast." In the bright sun, Willa's race was a shimmer of light and a small ruffling of the long grass.

"Willa!" Mrs. Dancourt looked over her shoulder with a disapproving frown. The old woman's voice was a sharp whisper. "You are being very rude. Odd Tom was just telling us about when automobiles came to town. Come and sit down."

Willa's bottom lip jutted out. She moved back to the broken fence.

"In a minute. It's Friday and the children will be leaving soon." Then she thought, "*They won't be back for two days.*" Even as Willa watched, the yellow bus pulled into the yard. Its squeaking door opened and all the children ran to get in line. Peter finally tagged Danielle as she stood with her big, pink paisley back-pack at her feet.

After the bus left, leaving only Mr. Tregenza to sweep up and lock the doors, Willa moved back to where the old ones were sitting. Pauline Savaria was talking about when Scarlet Fever came to town. Willa knew all about scarlet fever, she had been a little girl when she had gotten sick. The fever hurt her badly. Like many others, she had not been strong enough to live through the terrible pain. Now she lived here on Hurricane Mountain. She had been one of the last people to be buried here.

A new cemetery had been built near the highway. The new cemetery had nicely mowed lawns, stone benches for visitors to sit on, and a beautiful bell that tolled the hours. Here the grass was long; it hadn't been cut in years, and many of the small headstones had fallen down and were almost buried in the ground. No one came here to visit, not even Willa's parents. After she died, they had been sad and moved away from this village. She often wondered where they were now.

Willa was a Wisp, a tiny ghost child. She was the only child here with all the elders. Now she sat with them as they spoke about the things they remembered from living in the village. Odd Tom was talking about the automobiles again. He pronounced it *otter-mobiles*. Usually this made Willa laugh.

Mrs. Dancourt patted Willa's hand. Well, not patted, because wisps and ghosts are like smoke - their touch passes through whatever they reach for. They can't pick up anything, hold another's hand, or feel the sun on them. But they can glide through trees or dart in and out of the ground.

When Willa stood in the bright sun, no one could see her, but if one were looking just right one could see a shimmer in the light. At night or in the dark forest, anyone could see Willa. She looked like a wisp of steam coming off the top of a hot bowl of soup. The darker the day became, the better to see her but even then one could only see Willa if she wished. If she didn't want to be seen, she'd crinkle her nose, hunch her shoulders and *POP* out of sight. If you saw her today, tomorrow, or in a year, she always looked the same. Her long hair was tied with a big bow and she wore a drop-waist dress with small flowers on it and long sleeves. It had been her favorite and her last outfit.

"Is today almost All Hallow's Eve?" Willa asked Mrs. Dancourt.

"Shush," said Mrs. Dancourt.

Seated on the other side of Willa was Millie Saint Martin. She had worked at the general store all her life and was very friendly.

"Soon," Millie said. "Soon it will be Halloween and you can go into the village."

Willa sighed. She didn't listen to Odd Tom, she spent her time remembering the children running and playing.

When she had been at the Hurricane Mountain Cemetery for only a short time, she wandered down into the village looking for her parents. The summer day had been warm and bright, no one seemed to notice Willa. They walked right through her.

One person had shivered and said, "Ooh, goose

walked across my grave."

When Willa asked what that meant, the people standing there looked around for the child who had whispered. They couldn't see Willa, and her voice, soft like the wind, wasn't loud enough to be more than imagination. Everyone had laughed and walked away. Willa left the village.

Back at the cemetery Millie had found Willa behind the Mulberry Bushes. Tears like shiny orbs of water ran from Willa's eyes, disappearing when they dripped from her chin.

"Pretty sad, huh?" Millie asked.

Willa nodded, wiping at the tears with her sleeve. Millie decided it was time to explained to Willa what every young wisp needed to know.

"How about we talk about it?" said Millie, "There's some things for you to learn. Maybe a little story will cheer you up." When Willa nodded again, Millie scooted closer.

"Well, let's see," Millie began. "You know you can swoop through the trees and fly up into the sky for a little way. You know no one can see you and Odd Tom tells the same story over and over."

Willa laughed, which made Millie smile.

"Now let's talk about ghosts and people, living people." Willa and Millie sat side by side watching as nighttime crept in and the lights came on in the village, sparkling and twinkling, calling all the children home.

"Some people call us ghosts, or haunts, or spirits. We don't care. A little mite like you, you're a wisp. A sweet little wisp, but a wisp just the same. You can go anywhere; you don't have to stay here. Mostly we stay because really there is no place else for us to go. Every now and then a ghost or a wisp will go down to where the people are and they get seen. Well people, especially adult people are spooky. I mean, they are down right scary. They scream, they faint, they run away, and they tell other people about how terrible we are. Usually it's a lie. They teach the children to be afraid of us even though we can't do anything to hurt them."

"People are so scared of ghosts and so curious about them at the same time that on Halloween or as we used to call it, All Hallow's Eve, they dress up as ghosts. Yep, they do." Millie nodded at Willa, whose eyes were big and round as she listened to Millie.

"So, they're out there scaring each other, running around like they were playing tag, shouting 'BOO', and acting like they think we act. Have you ever heard one of us yell 'BOO'?"

"No," said Willa.

"Exactly," Millie continued. "Now, and this is

where you're going to like it, on Halloween while all this nonsense is going on, you can go down to the village. Nothing will change for you as long as you stay on the ground and don't let anyone touch you. No one is even going to notice you."

"Really?" Said Willa jumping up.

Millie motioned her back down to her seat.

"That's right. I go sometimes, well I used too." After that they sat quietly through the night and Willa waited for Halloween.

For several years after that Willa went down into the village on Halloween, but she was still lonely. The other children ran around with their friends while their parents followed. No one noticed her and no one offered to play. Willa stopped going to the village again. Now she watched the children while they played at school.

Between the cemetery and the school, running

down the mountain side was a thick pine forest. It grew all the way to the edge of the playground. When Mrs. Dancourt wasn't watching, Willa would drift down the hill and sit on a fallen tree where she could watch the children. The log had been there a long time and was melting into the earth. It was covered with soft green moss and had a sweet smell.

On Monday the children played baseball and Peter was at bat, Danielle was in right field. Willa sat on the log watching nervously. Peter was a strong boy. He walloped the ball sending it soaring over the head of all the other children and far past where Danielle stood. Then Peter was running the bases.

"Run, run Peter, run!" Shouted Willa. Although her voice sounded loud to her, it was only as noisy as the rustling leaves. Willa jumped up on the log, clasping her hands together hoping Peter could run fast enough not to get tagged. He stumbled, almost falling, Willa moved to the end of the log. Now she was floating a little higher.

Willa was so excited she didn't notice Danielle. When the ball had flown over her head and rolled into the forest, Danielle had chased after it. Now the little girl stood, ball and glove in hand, watching Willa's swirling dance of glee as Peter touched home plate. Spinning around, Willa jerked to a stop when she saw Danielle. Willa was so surprised she forgot to 'POP' and disappear.

"Hello," said Danielle.

"Hello," said Willa.

The teacher called to Danielle and the child turned to look. When she turned back again, Willa, who had remembered to POP, was gone. Though invisible, Willa watched Danielle look around a bit before running back into the schoolyard.

Later, sitting with the elders, Willa didn't dare tell even Millie what had happened, but she knew, she would go back to the schoolyard.

Every day after that Willa sat on the log. One day Peter brought his trucks to school, all the boys played in the sandbox building roads while the girls played on the swings and slide. Danielle walked back into the forest.

Willa sat without moving on the log, her hands pressed tightly together in her lap. She watched Danielle peer into the gloom until her eyes were accustomed to the greenish darkness. Danielle sat on the other end of the log, she also clasped her hands together.

"Hello," she said.

"Hello," Willa answered.

"I'm glad to see you again, I mean to really see you," Danielle said. She was very curious about everyone she met.

"Oh, and I am glad to see you." Willa wondered if she, if ghosts, could blush.

"How come you don't come to school?" Asked Danielle.

"Because I am a wisp." Willa worried that Danielle would scream, faint, or run away. Danielle sat looking at Willa.

"Don't you get lonely sitting here?" Asked Danielle.

"Yes, very lonely."

"Would you like to play? We could go back to the playground."

"I'd love to play, but I can't go to the playground."

"Hmm," said Danielle. "Well I could come here and play with you. I have dolls, do you have a doll?"

"No, I can't play with dolls," Willa said.

"Okay, what can you play?"

"I can play tag, I would be very good at tag," Willa smiled.

The school bell rang calling all the children back into school. Danielle stood up.

"Alright, I'll come back tomorrow and we'll play tag." Danielle waved good-bye and hurried back to the end of the line as the children marched into school.

Willa sat on the log until the bus left at the end of the day. "We'll play tag," she sang as she whooshed up the hill.

At home Danielle asked her mother, "What is a wisp?"

"A wisp," said her mother, "is a little bit of something."

"What if it's a person?" Asked Danielle.

"I guess it would be a small person," said her

mother reaching for the dinner plates.

"No mom, a person big as me, but maybe a little see-through."

Danielle's mother laughed as she handed the plates to Danielle. "Well if it's see-through, then maybe a ghost or a fairy."

"Fairies are tiny," Danielle said. She set the table, did her homework, and thought about Willa.

The next afternoon at recess Willa was sitting on the log, waiting. Danielle walked right up to her and asked, "Are you a ghost?"

"Yes," said Willa.

"But you are a wisp too?"

"I am called a wisp because I am a little kid ghost." Neither girl spoke, then Willa added. "I was very sick. My mom and dad did everything they could. Now I am a wisp." She paused. "You probably don't want to play with me now."

"No," said Danielle, "it's okay. Tag, you're it."

Throughout the autumn, Willa and Danielle played tag every day there was school. Willa would duck through a tree, and Danielle would yell, "No fair." Danielle would climb over logs, and Willa would copy the other girl's every move. When Halloween came, Willa went down into the village. She saw Danielle trick or treating with her parents and a small group of other children. Willa waved and Danielle waved back. All the way up the hill, Willa swirled in wispy circles, laughing and thinking about her new friend.

The cold days were coming. Danielle had on her new green winter coat. The girls sat side by side on the log. The snowflakes were falling.

"Aren't you cold, Willa?" Danielle asked.

"Oh no, I am never cold," said Willa.

"The bus is late today. We can play until it gets here," said Danielle, jumping to her feet.

"Yes!" Willa soared halfway up a tree.

"This time," Danielle said, "no cheating. No running through the trees." They ran until Danielle was exhausted. When the bus driver tooted the horn, they were deep in the forest.

"Bye, Willa," said Danielle, jumping over a log. Her foot slipped on the snowy surface and she fell backwards, landing with a hard thump on the ground.

"Danielle!" Willa slid through the log. She knelt next to her only friend. "Get up Danielle, the bus is here."

Danielle lay on the fallen leaves. Her eyes were closed. The snow was falling harder. Willa whooshed to the edge of the forest. She saw the bus door close.

"Wait!" She called. She hurried back to Danielle.

"Please Danielle, please get up." Willa tried to touch Danielle but her hand went right through her friend's arm. Willa went back to the forest edge. The bus was gone and the last car was pulling away. Through the big side windows of the school, Willa could see Mr. Tregenza carrying his mop and pail. She zoomed past the swings and through the wall.

"Mr. Tregenza," she called.

He stopped, listened to the whisper behind him, and turned slowly around. Willa floated about three feet away. Mr. Tregenza screamed and jumped backwards. He tripped over the mop bucket and fell down, but he did not faint. "Who are you?" he gasped.

"I am Willa," said Willa, floating closer, "and I need you."

Mr. Tregenza fainted.

Willa floated around the elderly man in frantic

circles. When his eyelids fluttered, she moved back a little bit and tried to be quiet. He looked around, his eyes wide with fright.

"Please do not faint, Mr Tregenza," Willa said. "I need you to help me. Danielle fell down in the woods and the bus is gone and the snow is falling. I do not know what to do." Mr. Tregenza crept backwards towards the principal's chair. When he was seated, Willa got a little closer. "Please, Mr. Tregenza, don't be afraid, Danielle needs you to help her."

"Who?" He said.

"Danielle, the little girl in the green coat."

Mr. Tregenza was making gasping noises trying to breathe. He kept shaking his head no. The phone rang. When he picked up the receiver, Willa could hear a woman's voice. "Who?" He said again.

"Danielle," said Willa. Mr. Tregenza was looking

out the window. Willa couldn't wait any longer. She zipped through the wall and rushed back toward Danielle. Through the glass, Mr. Tregenza could see a wispy girl of white disappearing among the snowflakes.

"Oh Danielle, I am so sorry." Willa knelt next to the other girl who was now nearly covered with snow. The tears glistening on Willa's cheeks froze then shattered into shiny bits of ice as they dripped off her chin.

In the distance Willa could hear a man and a woman calling Danielle, but she couldn't leave her friend again. Then closer she heard Mr. Tregenza.

"Willa," he shouted. "Willa."

"Here, here," she floated over to where he was tripping on branches, a flashlight in one hand and a blanket in the other. He followed her back to Danielle.

"She's here," he shouted. Other people came

crashing through the forest. Willa POPPED, but stayed among the trees watching as Danielle was bundled up and put in an ambulance. The ambulance drove away. Not back toward town but in the other direction, toward the bright shining lights of the big city.

Everyday Willa sat on the log, but Danielle did not come back. The next week a high chain link fence was put around the playground, so the children could not go into the forest. She sat silently watching Mr. Tregenza as he stood behind the fence. He did not call her, he could not see her, and she was afraid to speak to him. Finally Willa stopped going down the mountain. She did not sit with the others listening to Odd Tom. She stayed locked inside her old wooden grave marker. Millie stood outside and called to her. Willa would not come out and it was against the rules for Millie to go in.

Winter passed. The sun grew warm and shone on

Willa's grave marker drying the frost and melting the snow. Willa still did not come out.

"Willa," Mrs. Dancourt was calling. She sounded frantic. "Willa, quickly."

Willa stirred but did not go out.

"Willa!" Now Millie was calling. "Oh thunder," she said and stuck her head into Willa's grave marker. "You have got to come out right now. There's all these people here and a child is calling you."

Willa POPPED and went out. All the ghosts were invisible. They walked among the people who were there. Men were fixing grave markers. Mr. Tregenza was mending the broken fence. Women were planting flowers, and Danielle was kneeling in front of Willa's wooden grave marker.

"It's this one," Danielle said. "It says 'Willa'."

"Hello Danielle," Willa whispered.

"Oh Willa," Danielle reached out her hand toward the whisper. "I can't see you."

"I cannot POP," Willa told her, "with all these people here."

"Okay, but stay right with me," Danielle answered. "Over here Daddy, bring the angel over here." A tall man came toward them, pushing a wheelbarrow. Standing in the wheelbarrow was a beautiful stone angel, a little girl angel holding a lamb. The men took away the rough wooden grave marker laying it carefully near the fence. Then they moved the stone angel into its place. On the bottom were carved the words; "Willa, my friend."

"This is for you Willa," said Danielle, "so even when I am not here you will not be alone."

"Thank you," said Willa. "It is beautiful."

After that the days came and went. Danielle grew

to be a young lady but Willa always stayed a little girl. Danielle would come up Hurricane Mountain to visit Willa, and Willa would sit in the forest waiting for Danielle.

Mr. Tregenza, old and stooped, raked leaves away from the rusty chain link fence. In some places the fence was falling down, but no one cared anymore. A little girl with bright red hair stood near the fence gazing intently into the forest.

"Did you see that?" She whispered, then again louder. "Did you see that?"

"Huh, what's that?" Asked Mr. Tregenza moving closer.

"Did you see that flying star of light in the forest?" The little girl asked.

"I bet that flying star of light was like a wispy sort of cloud, swooping through the trees," Mr. Tregenza said.

The little girl nodded, never taking her eyes off the spot where the light had been.

"Well that girlie, that was Willa the Wisp." He leaned on the rake handle wiping his face with a big blue bandana. "Bet you don't know about wisps?"

The little girl shook her head no. Mr. Tregenza laughed, then dropped his rake and took her hand.

"Let's go find Miss Danielle in the school. We'll all sit down and she can tell you all about wisps, especially her friend, Willa the Wisp."

DonnaRae is a native of Vermont and lives in Northern New England. She enjoys reading, sewing, farmers markets and looking for incidental gems for her next book.

Made in the USA
Middletown, DE
11 February 2022

60289461R00020